D0399198

ESCAPE
from
SILVER STREET
FARM

ESCAPE
from
SILVER STREET
FARM

NICOLA DAVIES
illustrated by Katharine McEwen

CANDLEWICK PRESS

Text copyright © 2011 by Nicola Davies
Illustrations copyright © 2011 by Katharine McEwen

First U.S. edition 2013

Library of Congress Catalog Card Number 2012942620
ISBN 978-0-7636-6133-5

12 13 14 15 16 17 BVG 10 9 8 7 6 5 4 3 2 1

Printed in Berryville, VA, U.S.A.

This book was typeset in Stempel Schneidler and Cows.
The illustrations were done in pen and watercolor.

Candlewick Press
99 Dover Street
Somerville, Massachusetts 02144

visit us at www.candlewick.com

For Joseph and Gabriel,
Gem, Geraldine, and Gwenda

A MAP OF
SILVER STREET FARM

Main gate

FLORA'S OFFICE

FLORA'S VAN

Goats

Sheep

gate

Duck House

N

CANAL

Chapter One

Crash!

Scrunch!

Bash!

Kenelottle Mossworthy Merridale of Morrayside, Kenny for short, was *not* a happy ram. In fact, he'd been in a bad mood ever since he'd arrived at Silver Street Farm earlier in the day. Now the sheep was head-butting the door of his stall. In spite of the roar of the winter gale, the sound traveled all the way to the signal-box-turned-chicken-house, where Meera, Karl, and Gemma—the three friends who had founded the city farm—were shoveling chicken poop. Meera, who was strong and round, and Gemma, who was a bendy beanpole of a person, did the shoveling, while Karl, who was small and skinny, held a big sack open to catch the mixture of straw and poop. It was hard work—not to mention a bit smelly—and the children were glad to stop for a minute to listen to Kenny's temper tantrum.

"Now I know what a head banger really is!" said Meera.

"Won't he hurt himself?" asked Karl.

"No," said Gemma, the sheep expert

among them. "Their heads are like crash helmets. He'll settle down when he meets his wives later today."

Kenelottle Mossworthy Merridale of Morrayside's "wives" were Bobo and Bitzi, the Silver Street sheep. They had been sold to Karl's auntie Nat as poodle puppies when they were lambs and had turned out to be pedigree Shetland sheep, who in turn deserved a pedigree Shetland sheep husband: Kenny.

Meera plonked another dollop of poop-soaked straw into the sack. "Come on, guys," she said. "We'd better get this finished. There's a lot to do before tomorrow."

Meera was right. The next day was Christmas Eve, and Silver Street had to be ready for its grand opening. For the first time, the citizens of Lonchester would be able to visit their very own city farm. There were sheds to paint and repair and paths to clear, as well as all the day-to-day work like goat milking, sheep feeding, egg collecting, and poop clearing. But the children weren't daunted. They loved every minute of it (even the poop clearing). Silver Street Farm was their dream come true.

"Sometimes," said Gemma, heaving another smelly shovelful, "I have to pinch myself so I know I'm not dreaming."

"I know just what you mean," said Meera. "We spent so long *imagining* a farm like this, and now it's *real*."

"And when you think how it all started," Karl said with a laugh.

"Poodles that were sheep," said Meera.

"Rotten eggs that hatched into ducklings," said Gemma.

"The nicest policeman in the world," said Karl.

"And Flora!" they all said together.

Of all the lucky and amazing things that had helped them make their dreams of a farm in the city come true, the *most* lucky and amazing was Flora MacDonald. Flora, a young farmer from Scotland, had arrived out of the blue and offered to run Silver Street Farm. Flora's experience and hard work had turned a handful of animals and a ruined train station into a farm. She *was* a bit bossy sometimes, but she never forgot that Silver Street Farm was the *children's* idea — *their* dream.

"We've only got till tomorrow to get her a Christmas present," said Karl.

"Yeah," said Gemma. "But what? I can't see her going for scented soap and bubble bath!"

Meera smiled a knowing smile at her two friends.

"I've got an idea for Flora's present already," she said. "And it's a very, *very* good one. All we need to do is —"

But Meera didn't get the chance to say more, because just then Flora herself bounded up the wooden stairs to the chicken house, her curly hair blowing in the wind and her blue eyes blazing brightly.

"Action stations, you three!" she called in her broad Scottish accent. "Bitzi and Bobo are missing, and the turkeys have disappeared, too!"

Chapter Two

Silver Street turkeys had nothing to fear at Christmas. Their purpose in life was to show Silver Street visitors what live turkeys looked like, not to provide humans with yummy Christmas dinners. But, in spite of being some of the luckiest turkeys in the world, the Silver Street turkeys were nervous and flighty creatures. They paced up and down by the fence of their enclosure, as if looking for a way out. They gobbled in alarm every time anyone—

the children, Flora, or either of the two dogs (Buster, the Silver Street guard dog, and Flinty, Flora's chicken-herding sheepdog)— passed their pen and ran about with their wattles wiggling like strings of red licorice.

The turkeys' nervousness was starting to rub off on Bobo and Bitzi, the Silver Street sheep, in the next-door enclosure. Or rather, it was rubbing off on Bobo. (Nothing much at all rubbed off on Bitzi, who only really noticed two things: food and what Bobo was doing.)

Every time the turkeys gobbled or paced anxiously, Bobo headed for the far end of her pen. And because Bobo did, so did Bitzi. Pretty soon, they'd grazed almost all the grass and stray brambles that had covered the fence at that end. Which was how, on the day the children were merrily pitchforking chicken poop, Bobo and Bitzi nibbled through the last few bramble leaves covering the corner of their pen and found . . . nothing at all. No wire, no fence posts, just a gap.

Bobo stood and stared at the gap. It was scary and tempting at the same time. She turned her back and walked away, but the hole seemed to call to her. She soon found herself back beside it, staring through to the other side.

It was at that very moment that a large rat crossed the turkey pen, just as Buster was walking past on his way to look for cookie crumbs in Flora's van. Buster was big and fierce looking, but, in spite of his appearance and his previous job as a guard dog, he was a big softie. Except, that was, when it came to rats. *Especially* rats that swaggered as if they owned the place.

Grrrrrr! Buster flung himself at the fence, barking as loudly as he could. Rats, of course have a deep understanding of fences and know exactly when they are on the safe side of them. So the rat took no notice of Buster's woofs and snarls. The turkeys, however, already nervous for mysterious reasons of their own, had hysterics.

The nasty noise and commotion was all Bobo needed to overcome her fear of the unknown. She pushed her nose through the gap in the fence and pulled her fat, woolly bottom after it. Bitzi followed along dreamily with a bit of leaf sticking out of her mouth. They tip-tapped over the little metal footbridge to the other side of the canal and disappeared through a flurry of old newspapers and plastic grocery bags, which were suddenly caught up in a gust of wind like confetti. Behind them, the barking and gobbling suddenly stopped. With a lot of panicky flapping and another big gust of wind, the turkeys made it up, up, up and over the fence at the bottom of their pen, then immediately down, down, down on the other side and straight into the canal. The rat, no doubt pleased with the chaos it had caused, went back down its hole, and Buster trotted off, suddenly remembering the importance of cookie crumbs.

Chapter Three

It was easy to see how the sheep had gotten out—Karl and Flora found the gap in the fence at once. But when they searched along the canal bank, there was no sign of them.

"Could Flinty sniff them out?" Karl asked. "I mean, she *is* a sheepdog."

"She's *supposed* to be a sheepdog," Flora explained patiently, "but she's terrified of sheep. She's probably delighted that they're gone."

Hearing her name mentioned, Flinty wagged her tail and sniffed at the gap approvingly, as if to say "Nasty sheep, good riddance!"

"They could be miles away by now." Flora sighed and shook her head. "If they get onto a road, I dread to think what might happen."

Karl had never seen Flora so worried. He couldn't think what to say. Then he had an idea. "Could *Kenny* sniff them out?"

"That," said Flora, "is the craziest idea I've heard in a long while. . . . And it might just work. Although, he is a wee bit on the feisty side. . . ."

Kenny glared at Karl and Flora from the far end of his stall. He stamped his hooves and lowered his head, ready to charge with his beautiful curving horns. Karl decided that the only way the ram could look more impressive and scary was if he actually had fire coming out of his nostrils.

"The good thing about horns," said Flora quietly, "is that that they make good handles." Then she shook a bucket, and the sheep-food pellets rattled in the bottom.

Kenny raised his head and sniffed the air. He stopped stamping and walked daintily across the stall to bury his big head in the bucket and munch noisily.

"That's a good boy," said Flora. "OK, Karl. Now!" Gently but very firmly, they each took hold of one of Kenny's horns. The ram struggled furiously, making Karl's arm muscles scream for mercy. Then, after a few seconds, Kenny stood still and let Flora slip the halter over his head and secure it around his nose.

"There you go!" Flora said. "He's been in so many farm shows, he knows the routine of being on a halter and led about. He'll give us no more trouble now."

Kenny seemed pleased to be outside. He sniffed the wind and immediately set off down the ramp that led from the station platform to the sheep pen on the old train tracks. Karl and Flora didn't even have to guide the ram to the gap in the fence — he went straight to it, sniffed it carefully, then pushed through. He set off down the towpath and over the footbridge so fast that Karl and Flora had trouble keeping up.

"We'll find them in no time!" said Karl.

"I just hope they're not in any trouble," said Flora grimly. "We could do without any bad publicity before the grand opening."

Chapter Four

There was no sign of the turkeys anywhere, just a little whirlpool of feathers dancing in the wind. Meera and Gemma looked at each other, mystified.

"How can they have just disappeared?" said Meera. "They were here fifteen minutes ago."

"There must be some clue we're missing," said Gemma. "We've got to be like detectives. Come on, let's check the fences again."

The two girls split up and walked around the edge of the turkey pen, looking carefully at every bit of the fence.

Suddenly Gemma called out, "Hey, look at this!"

Where the pen bordered on a scrubby wasteland of grasses and brambles, a neat little door had been cut in the tall wire fence at ground level. It had been rejoined so cleverly that you had to look hard to see it. It would take just two or three twists of the wire closing the little door to open up a gap big enough to let a small child in—or ten turkeys out.

"Maybe someone came through and stole them," said Meera.

Gemma shook her head. "They'd have to catch them first, and you know how flighty our turkeys are," she said. "Flora told me that she heard them making a noise, and when she came out of the office a minute later, they were gone. There just wasn't time to catch ten turkeys and get them through this hole."

"Maybe it was the work of Gobble O Seven, international turkey thief," Meera joked, but they both knew it wasn't really funny. A grand opening with missing livestock was no laughing matter. Their only option seemed to be to go through the fence to see if there were more clues.

The gateway in the fence was smaller than it looked. Meera's bottom got stuck, and she ripped the seat of her jeans.

"Huh!" she muttered grumpily. "Well, at least we know we're looking for small, skinny turkey thieves!"

On the other side of the fence, there

was an old oil drum, and behind that was a tunnel through a tangle of plants. It was a tight squeeze, and Meera kept getting hooked up in brambles as she crawled along behind Gemma on her hands and knees, through a series of cold muddy puddles. The tunnel ran for more than a hundred yards and came out in a graveyard of old train equipment, out of sight from the farm.

"That's clever!" said Gemma. "Whoever made this tunnel knew they could crawl all the way up to the fence without being seen *and* make a quick getaway!" Gemma pointed to the wall at the end of the train cemetery. "The main road into town is on the other side of that wall."

"But how would you get ten turkeys through the fence, along the tunnel, and over the wall in less than half a minute?" said Meera, pulling herself free from a particularly thorny bramble. "Ten turkeys are really heavy, and there'd be loads of feathers everywhere."

Gemma shook her head. "Maybe," she said, chewing one of her braids thoughtfully, "this is a red herring."

"A what?" said Meera, pretty convinced that fish had nothing to do with missing turkeys.

"A red herring means a clue that isn't really a clue," Gemma replied. "You know, something that leads the detective off the real trail."

"So the hole in the fence and the tunnel might not have anything to do with how the turkeys disappeared this morning?" said Meera. "But if that's true, then I've just ripped my jeans for nothing!"

Gemma nodded. "I think," she said, "we need to go back to Silver Street Farm and allow chocolate cookies to fuel further investigations."

"That, Detective," Meera said, "is the smartest thing you've said all morning."

Chapter Five

Bobo sniffed the road. It smelled nasty: cold and oily and dead. There wasn't a scrap of anything to eat anywhere. None of the people were doing anything useful, like bringing them a nice bucket of food or half a bale of sweet hay. None of the humans they knew were there, just endless streams of strangers, who didn't seem to notice the two sheep at all.

Bobo tip-tapped closer to a huge doorway. A blast of warmth like summer wafted toward her, and Bobo moved closer, sniffing at the balmy curtain of air. There was a faint smell—a smell of something growing, something edible. Bobo trotted through the bright doorway with Bitzi close behind her.

It was certainly a very odd place. Bobo had never seen so many humans all together. They pushed wire carts like the ones she'd seen her humans pulling out of the canal. The floor was very hard and slippery, but it smelled a bit nicer than the road. The good thing was that there were buckets and boxes of nice edible things all around. They weren't arranged at the most convenient height for a sheep, which was irritating, not to mention inconsiderate, but Bobo had always been good on her hind legs.

Just above her nose was a bucket, very like her own feed bucket, stuffed full of leaves and flowers. Of course, being a sheep, she couldn't see the colors of the flowers, but she could smell their juicy smell. With a little jump, she lifted herself onto her hind legs and rested her dainty forelegs against the slippery bucket. It was rather uncomfortable, so she was glad when, as she tugged at the flowers with her mouth, the bucket of flowers, in fact *all* the buckets of flowers, began to fall. Deftly Bobo stepped out of the way and then stepped back to dig in to a feast so delicious that she didn't even notice the humans making a fuss all around her.

Bitzi had followed Bobo, as usual without

much thought, but she certainly woke up when she saw and smelled all the yummy stuff in buckets. In fact, she was so overcome by the sight and smell of so much exotic food that, as the flower stand keeled over, she didn't take the necessary avoiding action, and a large bucket plopped right over her head. Bitzi panicked. Who had turned off the lights so suddenly? Where had all that nice food gone? She trotted in circles, then realized that if she looked down, she could see her own familiar feet and, just a little farther on, the reassuring hooves of her leader.

At that moment, Bobo glanced over her shoulders and saw a monster with a huge square head and a sheep's body coming toward her. It was *horrible*. A beast with no eyes, clearly determined to eat her. She snatched one last flower stalk and fled over the slippery floor, scattering the screaming humans.

Kenny rounded the corner and went straight for the supermarket entrance, pulling Karl after him. The ram was really rather irritated now. Never, in all his long experience of ewes, had he encountered any as flighty as these two. He had followed their (admittedly very nice) smell for what seemed like hours, through all manner of horrible places completely unsuitable for any sort of sheep. And now they'd led him here, to this chaos, with humans running around and the floor covered in water and crushed plants.

There they were—those two naughty ewes—just up ahead, through the forest of human legs and supermarket carts. One of the foolish creatures had a bucket on her head. Dear me! It was up to him to sort this all out, right now! With a practiced and determined tug, Kenny jerked the halter leash free from Karl's hand, put his head down, and charged straight toward the two ewes, who were fast disappearing behind the breakfast cereals.

Chapter Six

By the time they'd gotten back to the Silver Street office, Meera and Gemma were covered in scratches from the bramble tunnel and freezing cold from crawling through muddy puddles. It had taken several mugs of tea and a large number of chocolate cookies to warm them up, but they were no nearer to solving the mystery of the disappearing turkeys. Just as they were wondering if another package of cookies might help, the phone rang.

"This is Silver Street Farm. Can I help you?" said Meera.

"Ah!" said a warm and booming voice down the phone line. "That's young Meera, isn't it?"

Meera grinned. It was Sergeant Short of the Lonchester Police Department. He'd been a great supporter of Silver Street Farm right from the start.

"Hello, Sergeant," said Meera. "I was just thinking of calling you. We think someone's stolen our turkeys!"

"Ah!" said the sergeant. "Well, in that case, you need to bicycle down to the Marston Park overflow dam, because I think your turkeys are about to go over it, riding on a bouncy castle."

"What?"

"There isn't time to explain," said Sergeant Short, "and I'm not really sure that I could anyway. Officer Worthing will meet you there."

Meera put the phone down. "Get your bike, Gemma," she said. "I'll tell you what we're doing on the way. Just follow me."

Meera knew the city well and she led Gemma through every shortcut possible. Pedaling furiously with their heads bent against the wind, the two girls raced into the parking lot nearest the dam just as Officer Worthing and her partner arrived in their police car. No one wasted time saying hello.

"I've brought some rope," said Officer Worthing. "I thought it might be useful."

"The gate to the bank's locked so you can't drive to the dam," said Gemma.

"We'll take the rope on the bikes," Meera told Officer Worthing. "Then you can catch up."

Seconds later, the girls each had a rope slung around their shoulders and were cycling down the towpath. As they rounded the last bend, where the canal joined the river and the water tumbled over the dam and down toward the sea, they saw the bouncy castle.

It was rather deflated but still afloat and turning around and around in the wind, looking like a cross between a soggy cake and a merry-go-round. In the middle, huddled in a heap between the checkered legs of an inflatable clown, were all ten turkeys, too tired now to make even the faintest gobbling sound. As the girls watched, the wind gusted and the castle picked up speed. In just a few moments, it would go over the dam and tip its feathery passengers into the white water!

"We need to get a rope around it somehow," said Meera desperately.

"That tree!" said Gemma, pointing to a huge old willow. "If we climb it, we can loop the rope around the clown as the castle goes past."

"What do you mean, 'we'?" growled Meera. "I'm no good at climbing."

"Practice makes perfect," said Gemma. She dropped her bike and ran toward the tree. "Come *on,* Meera!" she shouted.

The wind had dropped a little, so the castle wasn't moving quite as fast, but they still had very little time. Gemma quickly swung herself up into the old willow and began to squirm like a wriggling caterpillar along the branch that stuck out over the water.

"Hurry up, Meera!" she called.

"I'm not an acrobat like you!" Meera grumbled.

"Get on that low branch there," Gemma said. "Then I'll throw the rope to you through the clown's legs."

Meera didn't say anything. Gemma made it sound so easy, but even getting onto the "low" branch took all of Meera's courage. And to catch the rope, she would have to let go of the tree.

"Hurry, Meera!" Gemma's voice was high and urgent. The bouncy castle waltzed closer, and the sound of the dam roared in Meera's ears.

"Now!" Gemma yelled, and threw the rope.

Everything seemed to go into slow motion. The rope slowly uncoiled against the white winter sky. It passed under the arch of the clown's legs and headed down,

down toward Meera's outstretched hand. But at the last second, the wind picked up and cruelly jerked the rope aside. Meera could see that if she missed it, they were lost; the turkeys would be drowned, and the Silver Street Grand Christmas Opening would be a dismal failure. Nimbly as a trapeze artist, she crooked her legs over the branch and dropped upside down to hook the rope with the tip of her finger.

Time returned to its normal pace.

"Meera!" Gemma called excitedly. "That was *amazing*!"

It didn't feel amazing. It felt absolutely horrible to be hanging upside down by her legs, Meera decided.

"Gemma!" she wailed. "Can you help me get down?"

Officer Worthing and her rather worried-looking partner, Officer Owen, having finally opened the gate, came bumping along the bank in their police car as Gemma was helping Meera untangle herself from the tree branch. They helped the girls haul the bouncy castle to the bank and up onto dry land. The turkeys stayed sitting in a heap and allowed themselves to be picked up like so many soft, feathery cushions.

"Seasick, by the looks of it," said Officer Worthing.

"Well, they'd better not throw up or do *anything else* in the back of our car!" said Officer Owen as they bundled the tired turkeys into the police car, ready for their journey home.

But as they lifted the last of the turkeys, everyone froze. They gasped in astonishment, hardly able to believe their eyes. At the bottom of the turkey pile, warm as an egg under a chicken and fast asleep, was a baby.

Chapter Seven

Nobody minded about the chaos caused by the sheep in the supermarket. The manager even insisted on having his photo taken with Kenny and his two "girls," and the supermarket staff promised to sponsor Kenny's food for a year! The whole city seemed to think that it was a big Christmas love story. Rockin' Roland Rogers covered it on his afternoon show.

"Kenny the romantic ram crossed the city to find his true loves!" Lonchester's most famous DJ told his listeners.

In fact, Kenny's handsome face was all set to be front-page news until the story of the Great Turkey Baby Rescue broke.

"Baby Saved by Runaway Turkeys," said the *Lonchester Herald*.

"Silver Street Turkeys Save the Day," said the *City Gazette*.

"Trapeze Girl and Turkeys Save Baby from Drowning," said the *Daily Post*.

"Turkeys Keep Baby from Getting Stuffed!" said the *Lonchester Sun*.

Once again, Silver Street Farm was big news. Flora's office was full of reporters and cameramen, all wanting to talk to the children and take pictures of the turkeys, which were now safely back in their pen. Flora was delighted and handed out leaflets to every radio, TV, and newspaper reporter she could find, inviting them all to the grand opening on Christmas Eve.

"This is fantastic!" she said to the children. "Who would have thought the day would end like this?"

"Well, yes," said Gemma doubtfully. "But I still don't understand what really happened."

"Well," said Stewy, the cameraman from Cosmic TV who was an old friend of Silver Street, "Sashi knows the story, don't you, Sash?"

Sashi, the Cosmic TV reporter and another old friend, beamed at the children.

"I do!" she said. "And what a story! A bouncy castle in a backyard ten miles away from the city was caught in a freak gale. It blew three miles into another yard and knocked over a stroller. The baby fell out of the stroller and onto the castle. And the castle blew into the canal. The baby's mom had just dashed indoors to get her purse, and when she came out again, the stroller was tipped up and the baby was missing. She didn't see the castle because the wind had already blown it down the canal. No one put the missing baby and the missing castle together, so no one knew where the baby had gone."

"But what about the turkeys?" asked Meera.

"That's the easy part, isn't it?" said Sashi. "The bouncy castle got blown past your place just when the turkeys were flying over the fence."

"But I thought only wild turkeys could fly," said Karl.

"Maybe these turkeys are wilder than you thought," said Sashi. "Or maybe," she suggested, glancing at Buster, who was busy with some sandwich crumbs under Flora's desk, "something scared them."

The children still looked as if someone had told them that one and one no longer added up to two but made three and a half instead.

Sashi laughed. "You should see your faces," she said. "Haven't you three realized yet? This is just the kind of stuff that happens at Silver Street! It's going to keep Cosmic TV in stories for the rest of my career!"

Flora was also more than happy to accept

the series of bizarre coincidences that had filled the day. "The really important part," she said, "is that without our turkeys cozied up to his tiny body, that baby would have frozen to death. Our birds saved that baby's life! I've invited him and his parents to our grand opening. It's all good for Silver Street!"

At last, the news people left and the Silver Street crew had some time to themselves. Flora put the kettle on for tea, and they all sat around eating toast and cookies, and talking.

"Well," said Karl, through a mouthful of toast and butter, "if the turkeys can fly over the fence, then we need to make the fence higher."

"Or we need to make sure that nothing scares them," said Flora, giving Buster a disapproving look.

"You're forgetting what me and Meera found," said Gemma. "The hole in the fence and the hidden tunnel. We think someone's planning to steal our turkeys!"

"Maybe they've been planning to do it at night," Meera added, "when the turkeys are asleep and easy to catch."

"And there are just two nights left before Chistmas dinner," said Gemma.

"So we should keep watch all night tonight and tomorrow!" said Meera excitedly.

"Good plan!" agreed Karl.

"No," said Flora, groaning.

"Please," said the children.

"Och," Flora said with a smile. "Go and call your parents, or they'll think I've kidnapped you all."

Chapter Eight

The wind that had caused so much trouble that day had died away, leaving a clear sky. There were no streetlights at the old station, so Silver Street sat in a pool of moonlight.

From the window of the old waiting room, there was a clear view down into the turkey's pen, which was striped with silver light and black shadows. In the pen next door, Kenny posed in the light of the moon; he was much happier outside. Bitzi and Bobo were snuggled into the straw a few feet from the watchers, wondering why the humans were in their stall. A few of the bantams, who preferred sleeping with the sheep to sleeping with the other chickens, were perched on the old luggage racks, their feathers ruffled out against the cold.

"What time is it?" whispered Meera.

"Half past midnight," said Karl with a yawn.

In the nest of bales under the window, Flora snuffled in her sleep.

"She's knocked out," said Gemma. "You could tell us about her Christmas present now, Meera."

"OK," whispered Meera. "Well, my uncle Sanjay—"

But, once again, Meera was interrupted.

"Shhhh!" hissed Karl. "Look!"

Somebody was crouching at the end of the grass tunnel and opening the hidden wire gate into the turkey's pen. The children withdrew into the deep shadow beside the window and waited.

Two very small figures wriggled through the fence and climbed up the ramp to the stall next door, where the turkeys were shut in at night. The children could no longer see the intruders from the window, but they could hear the sound of a bolt being carefully drawn back. A moment later, flashlight shone through the cracks in the boards that separated the sheep's quarters from the turkeys'. Quiet as ghosts, the children crept across to the wall so they could spy on the turkey rustlers.

The flashlight showed two boys. One was

very small and one a little bigger, and both had the same button noses and straight-set mouths. The children recognized them at once. The boys had belonged to a group from the youth club run by Sergeant Short. He'd brought them for a visit to Silver Street a month ago. Meera remembered how the button-nosed brothers had asked a *lot* of questions about turkeys.

The bigger boy was inspecting the turkeys as they perched in a line with their heads under their wings, fast asleep. Very gently, he stroked their backs and the feathers on their chests, then finally returned to the third one in the row.

"I think that one's the biggest," said the older boy. "Get the bag ready, Squirt."

The smaller boy unfolded a large sack and held it open.

"Won't the turkey wake up, Bish Bosh?" he asked his older brother.

"Not after I've stretched its neck!" said Bish Bosh.

"What?" Squirt's little voice piped higher in shock. "You're going to kill it?"

"Well, it can't be alive when we eat it, Squirt."

Squirt's head dropped to his chest, and he began to cry. Bish Bosh sighed, bent down, and put his arm around his little brother.

"What did you think we did all this for?" he asked gently.

Squirt just shook his head.

"I thought we were taking one to be my pet!" he wailed.

"Shh," said Bish Bosh. "Somebody'll hear us!"

But it was too late—somebody had. Flora woke up suddenly and shouted, "Wassthat?" loudly enough to be heard halfway across the city.

"Run!" Bish Bosh told Squirt.

Meera, Karl, and Gemma dashed out of the sheep stall to give chase. The turkey rustlers had a crucial two second head start, but in their panic they went down the wrong ramp. Instead of running into the turkey pen, with its door to freedom, the boys ran into the sheep pen, where Kenny was pacing about in the frost.

As far as Kenny was concerned, these were two more flighty young creatures that needed a lesson. Like a Spanish bull, he put his head down and charged.

Bish Bosh heard the hooves on the frosty

ground and saw Kenny. He scooped up Squirt and boosted him to safety on the duck-house roof, then, just in time, scrambled up after him. The turkey rustlers were trapped.

Squirt and Bish Bosh were far too little to be allowed to find their own way home in the middle of the night, Flora said. But, since the boys wouldn't tell her anything about where they lived or who their parents might be, she called the police.

Sergeant Short, who had just come back on duty, seemed to know exactly who Squirt and Bish Bosh were and came himself in a squad car to take them home.

Chapter Nine

The moon was still shining when Flora got up the next morning. Frost sparkled everywhere in the last of the moonlight and the first glow of dawn. It was going to be a perfect day.

She let the sheep and the ducks and the turkeys out and gave them their breakfast. The goats didn't need milking in the morning at this time of year, so she let them wander out, too. Then she took Flinty and Buster to wake the sleepy children, who had spent what was left of the night on the three old sofas in the office. With a combination of nose licking and jumping on heads, the dogs had soon woken them up.

"Come on," Flora said. "You never get the chance to see the dawn on your farm, because you don't live here. Come and look."

She led Meera, Gemma, and Karl across the yard and up to the old signal box, where the chickens were clucking to be let out. She ran up the steps to open the door, and the bantams fluttered down in a feathery fall while the big hens jumped down the steps.

"Now," said Flora, "come up here."

The children climbed the steps to the signal box, and they all looked out from the top, over the whole of Silver Street Farm.

Flora's timing was perfect. Behind them, the sun tipped over the lip of the city and flooded the whole of the old station with golden light. All the animals and birds in their neat pens were laid out below them like a toy farm. In the rich morning light, the colors glowed. The creamy white of the sheeps' fleece turned gold, while the turkeys shone like copper, their red wattles as bright as holly berries. Flinty's black-and-white fur looked painted as she practiced her chicken herding. Buster's black coat gleamed like polished wood. Even the browns and grays and reds of the goats and chickens looked like silk embroidery.

"Wow!" Karl breathed.

"Yeah!" Gemma said. "Wow!"

Meera hugged Flora. "You did this!" she said.

"I did not!" exclaimed Flora, leaning down a little to look intently into all their faces. "You three imagined your city farm, and you kept imagining it, and *that's* what did it."

They were all quiet for a moment as they looked at the scene.

Then Flora said quietly and almost to herself, "This is just the start. Next year, a cow, maybe. And pigs. Oh, pigs *would* be nice!"

As Flora stared dreamily into the distance, Gemma noticed that Meera was smiling rather knowingly to herself.

"*What?*" Gemma mouthed at her silently.

"*Tell you later,*" Meera mouthed back.

That was the last quiet moment of the day. The official grand opening was at three p.m., and there was still lots to do. Flora got busy finishing off the special Christmas goats' milk cheeses she'd been making. This left the children free to get on with the Christmas decorations: streamers made from the ivy that grew on most of the buildings, feathers painted gold, and little wooden chicken shapes that Karl had been secretly making all semester in wood shop.

Finally Meera had the chance to tell Karl and Gemma about Flora's two special Christmas presents.

"Uncle Sanjay's bringing them tonight," said Meera.

"Right," said Karl. "We'd better get to work. They'll need somewhere to live."

So, while Flora was safely out of the way in the dairy, the three friends spent the rest of the morning clearing trash and weeds from the old brick toolshed and its little yard.

"If Flora asks what we're doing, we can just say that we wanted it to look tidy for opening day," said Gemma.

"Yeah," said Karl. "She won't notice the feed and water buckets tucked behind the wall!"

At lunchtime, other helpers began to arrive with all sorts of contributions for the grand opening. Auntie Nat had used Silver Street eggs to make lots of beautiful golden challah bread, and Meera's mom had made Indian sweets—*jalebi, gajar halwa,* and *singori*. The food looked like plates of jewels.

"Next year when I make these," Meera's mom said, "maybe I'll be able to do it with milk from a Silver Street cow, right?"

Stewy, the cameraman from Cosmic TV, popped in with a huge pile of little green fritters. "I'll be back later to do a report, but I wanted to help out, too," he said. "These are Jamaican callaloo fritters. My mom taught me how to cook them."

At last, Flora emerged from the dairy with a tray of tiny round cheeses, each one decorated with a nettle leaf and tied with a band of red ribbon, and arranged them with the rest of the goodies. The tables in the office—made from two old doors balanced on trestles—were now covered in dishes of yummy party food.

"It looks gorgeous!" said Flora.

At half past two, Sergeant Short turned up. The children almost didn't recognize him out of uniform. He'd brought a large Christmas cake and two surprise guests: Bish Bosh and Squirt. The brothers were both freshly scrubbed and looked nervous.

"We've come to say that we're sorry," said Bish Bosh in a very small voice.

"Yes," said Squirt, so quietly that nobody actually heard him.

At last, Bish Bosh found the courage to look up. "The thing is," he said, "we'd like to help out. On your farm. Please."

There was a long pause, then Flora smiled. "Consider yourselves hired, boys," she said. "You've clearly got a way with livestock. Shake on it, eh?"

Chapter Ten

The farm looked almost as beautiful at sunset as it had at dawn. The fences were all in good order, the paths were swept, and the animals were on their best behavior.

Everything and everyone was ready for the grand opening. Buster and Flinty greeted everyone most politely by wagging their tails and offering their paws. Flora and the children showed the many visitors around, while various reporters and film crews pointed cameras and microphones at almost everything—but especially at the turkeys and Kenny. Everyone seemed to love it all.

Then the Turkey Rescue Baby, whose name was Ralph, arrived with his mom and dad, and there was another flurry of cameras and lights. Ralph's mom burst into tears when she saw the turkeys and again when she spoke to the children. Ralph's dad didn't say much at all, just pressed a fat envelope stuffed with money into Flora's hands before they took Ralph home to bed.

Bish Bosh and Squirt helped out with the evening chores by feeding and watering the animals. Already they seemed part of the team.

As it got dark, the children lit candles in jam jars and put them all around the farm, lighting the paths and the pens and the buildings. Silver Street Farm gleamed like a fairy tale.

The grand opening turned into a party. Mr. Khan, who owned the corner shop, had brought his trombone, and Gemma's dad his accordion. Together, they began playing every old tune they could think of. Everyone sang along between mouthfuls of food.

And then, just as Meera was wondering if Uncle Sanjay was going to let her down, his old white van trundled into the yard. Flora was talking to Sashi, so luckily she didn't notice the van arriving or the children slipping away.

Ten minutes later, Meera, Gemma, and Karl climbed onto an old sofa and stood together in a line. Meera tapped a glass with a fork to get everyone's attention. "Ladies and gentlemen," she said, "thank you all for coming to this grand opening."

"As I'm sure you know," said Gemma, "Silver Street Farm would not be ready for its first visitors without Flora MacDonald."

Everyone cheered.

"And," said Karl, trying hard to speak up in spite of his nervousness in front of so many people, "Meera, Gemma, and I would now like to give Flora her Christmas present."

Right on cue, Mr. Khan and Gemma's dad struck up "Old MacDonald" and everyone trooped outside, with jam-jar lanterns lighting their way. The children led Flora and the guests to the newly refitted tool shed.

There were lanterns all the way around the

wall, and, in the little yard, happily chomping their way through some chopped cabbage mixed with whey from Flora's cheese making, were two lovely spotted pigs.

Flora was astonished—and very pleased.

"They're just wonderful!" she said. "Gloucester Old Spots—my favorite breed. How on earth did you get them?"

"Well," said Meera, "that's my uncle Sanjay, over there." Uncle Sanjay waved shyly from the back of the crowd. "He was installing a new boiler in a farm in the country . . ."

"And he mentioned that his niece was part of the *famous* Silver Street Farm . . ." said Karl, taking up the story that Meera had finally told them that morning.

"And the man said he could have two of his young sows . . ." continued Gemma.

"And Uncle Sanjay brought them here in his van!" Meera said, completing the tale.

Everyone laughed and cheered. Flora hugged the children and Meera's uncle. Gemma was sure that she was about to hug the pigs, too, when the sound of high clear voices singing a carol made everyone suddenly quiet.

Without a word, Flora, the children and the whole crowd of visitors tiptoed toward the sound, which came from Kenny's pen, where the ram was spending the night outside as usual. There, sitting in a pool of candlelight, were Bish Bosh and Squirt, looking for all the world like a pair of little angels. They were singing:

"In Bethlehem did shepherds keep
Their flocks of lambs and feeding sheep . . ."

Their voices blended sweetly, as brothers'

voices often do. The boys looked up at the people gathered along the edge of the old platform and grinned, but they weren't singing for the Silver Street visitors. Their real audience was Kenelottle Mossworthy Merridale of Morrayside. The ram stood still, no longer grumpy or aggressive, with his big head resting on Bish Bosh's knee, and his eyes peacefully shut, soothed by the voices of the boys he'd been so eager to chase.

"Silver Street magic strikes again!" whispered Sashi. "I can't wait to see what next year will bring!"

SILVER STREET FARM
The Little Farm in the Big City

Some surprise ducklings, poodle puppies that turn out to be lambs, and a very stubborn goat — what more do three determined kids need to open a city farm? A friendly policeman, some singing supporters, and a dog that herds chickens, of course!

Join in the fun, feathers, and furry mayhem down on Silver Street Farm.

WELCOME TO

SILVER STREET

FARM

Nicola Davies   illustrated by Katharine McEwen

NICOLA DAVIES has a degree in zoology and is the author of many nonfiction books for young readers, including *Gaia Warriors, Poop,* and *Just the Right Size*. The Silver Street Farm stories mark her short-fiction series debut. About the series, she says, "I don't remember a time when I wasn't utterly besotted with animals." She lives in Wales.

KATHARINE McEWEN has illustrated more than twenty-five books, including Allan Ahlberg's *The Children Who Smelled a Rat* and Phyllis Root's *Here Comes Tabby Cat* and *Hey, Tabby Cat!* She lives in London.